Fly, Bessie, Fly

BY LYNN JOSEPH   ILLUSTRATED BY YVONNE BUCHANAN

Simon & Schuster Books for Young Readers

SIMON & SCHUSTER BOOKS FOR YOUNG READERS
An imprint of Simon & Schuster Children's Publishing Division
1230 Avenue of the Americas, New York, New York 10020
Text copyright © 1998 by Lynn Joseph
Illustrations copyright © 1998 by Yvonne Buchanan
SIMON & SCHUSTER BOOKS FOR YOUNG READERS
is a trademark of Simon & Schuster.
Book design by Lucille Chomowicz
The text for this book is set in Bernhard Modern.
The illustrations are rendered in watercolor and pen-and-ink.
Printed and bound in the United States of America
First Edition 10 9 8 7 6 5 4 3 2 1

Library of Congress Cataloging-in-Publication Data
Joseph, Lynn.   Fly, Bessie, fly / written by Lynn Joseph ;
illustrated by Yvonne Buchanan. p.   cm.
Summary: A brief biography of the woman who, in 1921,
became the first African American to earn a pilot's license.
ISBN 0-689-81339-2
1. Coleman, Bessie, 1896-1926—Juvenile literature.
2. Afro-American women air pilots—Biography—
Juvenile literature. [1. Coleman, Bessie, 1896-1926. 2. Pilots.
3. Afro-Americans—Biography.
4. Women—Biography.] I. Buchanan, Yvonne, ill. II. Title.
TL540.C646J67 1998 629.13'092—dc21 [B] 97-27304

In Waxahachie, Texas, 1901, it seems as if the cotton fields stretch from the ground right up to the sky. The fat white cotton bolls wait under the hot sun for dark hands to pluck them off their stems and place them in cool bags.

In the middle of this whiteness stands nine-year-old Bessie Coleman, her arms spread wide like the wings of a brown bird ready to fly. A bag of cotton weighs heavily on one shoulder. Bessie puts it down and spins around and around. She tilts her head back to look up into the center of the blue sky.

"Far away, far away,
Up past the clouds.
High away, fly away,
And never come down," she sings.

"Bessie, stop that daydreaming and come on!" calls Ma, who has stopped to wipe her brow.

Bessie looks down at the whiteness around her. Picking cotton makes her hands sticky with sweat. She squirms at the dirt settling deep into her skin and hair. She hitches the bag back on her shoulder, higher this time, and glances up once more at the sky's cool blue freedom.

"You talking to the birds, Bessie?" asks her little sister, Georgia.

"To myself," says Bessie as she trudges after Ma.

At the weigh-in station, Bessie's bag is only half full.

Ma sighs. "Ain't no cotton in heaven, Bessie. So staring up there ain't going to get the work done."

Bessie knows that Ma isn't angry with her. Most likely she's upset because of Pa, Bessie tells herself.

Bessie's father, George Coleman, is almost a full-blooded Indian. He just left home to go and live in the Indian Territory of Oklahoma. Now Bessie's mother, Susan Coleman, is raising her children alone.

Ma can't be too mad at me, Bessie decides. I'm the one who can do the figuring so that we get every penny we earn for every pound of cotton we pick.

As Mr. Jackson weighs Ma's bag, Bessie eyes it carefully. "You figuring that right, Mr. Jackson?" asks Bessie. "Looks like Ma's bag should be more."

"You getting too smart for the likes of me, Miss Bessie," Mr. Jackson teases. "When is that colored school opening back up so that I can count my money in peace?"

"Two more days," says Ma. "Right after the harvest."

Bessie loves the lessons in school, but every year the schools for black children are closed until all the cotton is harvested. The schools for white children open on time, as always.

Bessie ducks her head at the proud smile on Ma's face. Bessie feels as if she can truly fly, far away from the cotton fields.

Sometimes, Bessie thinks that picking the cotton bolls will never end.

But one day all the work is done.

"Time for some fun," says Ma.

The circus is in town, and Ma gives the girls each a shiny half-dollar to spend as they please.

At the fairgrounds, Bessie and Georgia can't stand still for a minute.

"Bessie, look at those pink clouds," shouts Georgia. "And those red candy apples."

Bessie laughs. They each buy a pink cloud and stand in line to buy their tickets for the show.

"This tastes like a fluffy cloud dipped in honey," says Georgia.

"Like sweet fairy dust," says Bessie.

The ticket line is long, stretching all the way around the circus tent like a desert rattlesnake. There are two other ticket booths open with shorter lines. But they have signs on them: WHITES ONLY.

Just then, Bessie and Georgia hear loud squeals from inside the circus tent. A voice booms: "Ladies and gentlemen, boys and girls, welcome to the circus."

"Bessie, the show is getting ready to start," cries Georgia. "We're going to miss it."

"Come on," says Bessie as she takes Georgia's hand. Together they walk up to one of the ticket booths where no one stands in line.

Bessie puts her money on the counter. "May we please have two tickets for the show?"

The ticket man shakes his head and points to the sign. Georgia begins to cry.

Bessie turns to her little sister. "Don't you dare cry, Miss Georgia Coleman," she says firmly. "You know what Ma tells us. We are all born the same under God's eyes. Them little signs don't mean anything to us, you hear me?"

Bessie raises her head high as she walks back to the other line.

"Besides," says Bessie, stretching her arms wide, "I'm a bird flying high above the circus. I can see everything, and it sure looks fine."

"What do you see, Bessie?" asks Georgia.

"I see big African elephants and bright red clowns," says Bessie.

Georgia flaps her arms. "I see the elephants, too, Bessie. And jungle tigers with stripes."

"Come on, Georgia. Fly with me right out of Waxahachie. Good-bye, Waxahachie," shouts Bessie, flapping her arms hard.

Georgia flaps her arms as mightily as she can, but she can't keep up with Bessie.

By the time Bessie grows to be a woman, no one can keep up with her. In 1915, at the age of twenty-three, Bessie decides to head to the North for the city of Chicago, where her older brothers, Walter and John, live. Walter is a Pullman train porter. John works at whatever jobs he can find, sometimes as a cook or a janitor.

Bessie boards the Rock Island train to Chicago. "I want to do something great!" she tells Ma and her sisters as they say good-bye at the station.

All her life growing up in Texas, Bessie has held fast to one dream: to amount to something. She doesn't know what she will do, but she knows it will be something special and different. As Bessie waves from the train window, the cotton fields of Waxahachie slip far behind. The train wheels begin to hum:

> *Far away, far away,*
> *Up past the clouds.*
> *High away, fly away,*
> *And never come down.*

Bessie listens to her song almost all the way to her new home.

To Bessie, Chicago is a city of dreams. Here, she is far away from the Jim Crow laws of the South—laws that tell Bessie she can't eat, drink, or ride in the same places as whites. Bessie does not know that even in the North, people with skin the darker shades of heaven are not always considered people at all.

Still, on Chicago's South Side, where Bessie's brothers live, Bessie finds big-city excitement. She works all day at the White Sox barber shop on the Main Stroll. She manicures men's hands and listens closely to their fancy talk about politics, banking, and music.

After work, Bessie loves to dress up and go to clubs such as the Pekin Café and Dreamland. She listens to Louis Armstrong, Bessie Smith, and Ethel Waters, some of the best black performers of the day. She dances the night away to songs that make her feel as if she's soaring free as a bird.

But Bessie misses her family back home, too. She writes them letters to tell them about her new life.

Dear Ma,

I am meeting some great people. My hero is Robert Abbott. He is a famous black publisher who knows everyone and everything. He owns the *Chicago Defender*, a black newspaper. Mr. Abbott gives speeches all over the South Side. He says "Black people must uplift themselves. We must each aspire to be somebody." I met him at one of his talks in town and I told him that I plan to uplift *myself*.

Love, Bessie

But Bessie often stays awake at night thinking and wondering, *How* will I uplift myself?

Then in April 1917, the United States enters World War I, and Bessie's thoughts turn to the safety of her brothers. Both Walter and John enlist with the Eighth Army National Guard, an all-black outfit that goes to fight the war in France. Every day, Bessie reads the newspapers to find out about her brothers and the war. She reads stories about the daring heroics of airplane fighter pilots. She sees photographs of these aviation heroes. When her brothers return, John tells Bessie that some of these heroes are women pilots.

"They fly airplanes just like the men," exclaims John. "Ain't no black woman could ever do that," he teases Bessie.

But Bessie does not smile. "That's it," she whispers to her brothers. "That's what I'm going to do. I'm going to fly—just like the birds."

John shakes his head. He doesn't believe Bessie. But Walter encourages her. "Fly, Bessie, fly!"

Bessie's dream of flying is halted by one big problem. No one in Chicago—in fact, no one in the United States—will teach her how to fly a plane.

Instead, people laugh at her. "Colored folks can't fly planes," some say.

And others remark, "Are you crazy? Colored women are cooks and maids, not pilots."

Bessie doesn't listen. She turns to Mr. Abbott. "Where can I learn to fly a plane?" she asks him.

"You will have to go to France, Bessie," he tells her. "The French are leaders in aviation and, more importantly, they will teach you how to fly."

"France!" Bessie exclaims. "But that's so far away. I..." Bessie stops just in time. She has almost said the one thing her mother has forbidden her to utter: "I can't."

"Okay, Mr. Abbott, I'll go to France," declares Bessie.

Bessie makes a list of all the things she will have to do:

1. Work hard.
2. Save money.
3. Learn to speak French.

Every day, Bessie gets closer to her dream. She finds a new job as the manager of a chili restaurant, and she earns more money. She puts her money in the bank. She takes French lessons at night school.

Finally, one day, Bessie says, "I'm ready to go." This time, instead of a train, she will be sailing to a new world on a ship. Bessie thanks Mr. Abbott for his help.

"When you come back, my paper will do a big story on you, Bessie," he promises.

She hugs Walter and John good-bye. "Look for me in the skies," she tells them.

On November 20, 1920, when the S.S. *Imparator* sails out of New York City's port, Bessie Coleman is aboard, headed for France. As everyone on the ship waves good-bye to their friends and family, Bessie looks up at the wide ribbon of sky that is leading her to her dream.

She sees birds flying overhead. They seem to be flapping their wings in time to her song of long ago:

> *Far away, far away,*
> *Up past the clouds.*
> *High away, fly away,*
> *And never come down.*

"I'm going to be a flier, just like you," she whispers.

In France, Bessie can't keep her eyes off the stylish suits and dresses that the men and women wear. She struggles with the French words that sound so strange to her ears, even when she herself is saying them. But none of that matters when Bessie begins her flying lessons at the *Ecole d'Aviation des Frères Caudron*. The first time she sits behind the controls of a plane, she trembles with excitement.

Dear Ma,

I am so happy. I flew with my teacher today in a French Nieuport biplane. I am learning how to do tailspins, banking, and looping the loops. I am truly flying with the birds now.

Love, Bessie

One of the greatest days in Bessie Coleman's life arrives seven months later. It is June 15, 1921, and Bessie passes the *Fédération Aéronautique Internationale* test for her pilot's license. Her dream of freedom high above the cotton fields has finally come true.

Dear Mr. Abbott,

They tell me I am the first black woman in the world to earn a pilot's license. And the first black American to do so. I can't stop staring at my photograph on my license. Is it really me, Bessie Coleman, a pilot-aviator? Thank you for all your help.

Love, Bessie

Bessie returns to the United States on the S.S. *Manchuria* in September 1921. Instantly, she is a star. Everyone wants to take the picture of the only black woman aviator in the world. Newspaper reporters ask her, "Why do you want to fly, Bessie?"

Bessie answers firmly, "We must have aviators if we are to keep up with the times. I would like to open a school to teach flying to the black men and women of this country."

In order to start a flying school, Bessie needs to raise money. She becomes a barnstormer pilot, flying in air shows around the country. Everywhere she goes, people come to see a black woman fly a plane. But Bessie does not have her own plane. In each city where she performs, she must borrow a plane to perform her special twists and daring turns that thrill the audience.

One air show on October 15, 1922, is Bessie's most important performance. It is held at the Checkerboard Airdrome in her beloved city of Chicago. Folks come from near and far—Ma, Georgia, and Bessie's brothers, Walter and John.

An audience of over two thousand spectators, both black and white, gathers to see Bessie soar with the birds. Bessie waves to her family as she walks to the plane. Then she takes off down the runway with a roar. She lifts the airplane up into the sky and smiles at the loud cheering she hears below.

"Far away, far away,
Up past the clouds.
High away, fly away,
And never come down," she sings as she soars higher and higher.

Then Bessie looks through the parted clouds. Far below she sees the most beautiful sight.

"Ma was right," she whispers as she gazes down at the people of the city. "We are all born the same under God's eyes."

AUTHOR'S NOTE

Born on January 26, 1892, in Atlanta, Texas, Bessie Coleman lived the life of a true adventurer. Her career as a stunt pilot took off after a few shows. The *Chicago Defender* nicknamed her "Queen Bess." Other newspapers referred to her as "Brave Bessie" because of her calm control during dangerous stunts. Bessie finally bought her own plane in January 1923, a year and a half after earning her pilot's license. It was a World War I Curtiss JN-4, a "Jenny" biplane. Bessie and her Jenny performed daredevil stunts in several air shows before tragedy struck.

At a Southern California air show only a couple of months after buying the Jenny, Bessie's plane crashed. Bessie was taken to the hospital with broken ribs and a broken leg. Many believed this was the end of her flying career. But Brave Bessie couldn't wait to get back in the skies. In a telegram message to the press, she wrote: "Tell them all that as soon as I can walk, I'm going to fly!"

Two years later, Bessie was fully healed and the star of an air show that toured the South. One of the shows was in Waxahachie, Texas. But in 1925, Texas was still governed by the Jim Crow laws that Bessie despised.

Bessie's 1925 tour was successful, and she had almost enough money to open her flying school. But first, she decided to perform in a few more air shows in Florida. One show was for the Negro Welfare League in Jacksonville, Florida.

During a test flight early on the morning of April 30, 1926, Bessie Coleman took to the skies for the last time. A mechanical failure caused her Jenny plane to dive straight down, and Bessie was thrown out of the plane and killed.

Over ten thousand people came to honor Brave Bessie Coleman, America's first black pilot, at her burial in Chicago's Lincoln Cemetery.

Bessie's spirit lives on today. Every year on the date of her death, pilots from all over the country fly over Lincoln Cemetery to drop flowers on her grave.

BIBLIOGRAPHY

Hart, Philip S. *Up in the Air: The Story of Bessie Coleman*. Minneapolis: Carolrhoda Books, 1996.

Johnson, LaVerne C. *Bessie Coleman*. Empak "Black History" Series. Chicago: Empak Enterprises, 1992.

Rich, Doris L. *Queen Bess: Daredevil Aviator*. Washington: Smithsonian Institution Press, 1993.

Yount, Lisa. *Women Aviators*. New York: Facts on File, 1995.